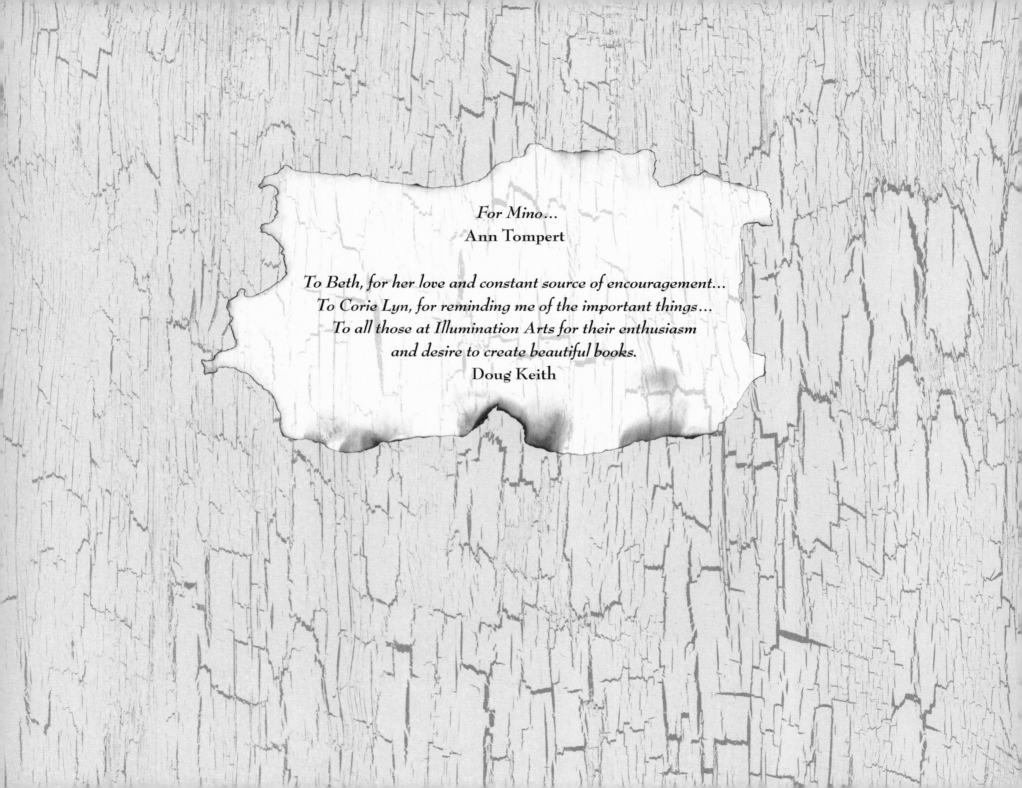

For Mino...
Ann Tompert

To Beth, for her love and constant source of encouragement...
To Corie Lyn, for reminding me of the important things...
To all those at Illumination Arts for their enthusiasm
and desire to create beautiful books.
Doug Keith

THE ERRANT KNIGHT

STORY BY ANN TOMPERT

**ILLUSTRATIONS BY
DOUG KEITH**

ILLUMINATION Arts

PUBLISHING COMPANY, INC. ◆ BELLEVUE, WA

nce long ago, when the year was greening with spring, a brave knight was called to serve his King. "His Majesty is but a boy like you," the knight told his squire who was loading a mule with supplies. "He may need much help."

"Will you be fighting giants?" asked the squire.
"If the King commands me," said the knight.

"Will you be slaying fire-breathing dragons and saving beautiful maidens?" asked the squire.

"I will not be an *errant* knight, wandering about seeking adventure," said the knight as he adjusted the golden spurs sent to him by the King.

Without delay, he mounted his horse
and set out at a lively pace.

The knight had not gone far when he came upon a group of travelers gathering baggage strewn about the roadside.

"Thank God, who in His goodness sent you this way," said a wool merchant. "We were set upon by robbers who rode off with our horses when they saw you coming."

"We are afraid to go on," said the merchant's daughter, "and we are afraid to stay. But if you joined us, we would surely be safe."

"Where do you go?" asked the knight.

"North to Leeds," said the merchant.

"Alas, I go south," said the knight. "I cannot help you, for I have been called to serve our King."

When the travelers surrounded his horse
and held on to his saddle, the knight frowned.
"What right have you to delay me with your
problems?" he asked. "I am not an *errant*
knight, roving aimlessly about the countryside."

But the fear and hope on the travelers' faces robbed the knight of any choice. So together they journeyed for many days—through villages and towns, fields of sprouting grain, sunny meadows with grazing sheep, and dark, foreboding forests—until at last the wayfarers reached their destination.

Without stopping to rest, the knight again set out for the royal castle. But as he was picking his way along a path, his horse's reins caught on a branch. When he tried to yank them loose, one snapped in half.

In a nearby village, the knight stopped at a leatherworker's shop where he found a woman pacing and wringing her hands.

"My husband is with the village men looking for Bonnie, our wee one," said the woman. "She wandered off into the forest and no one has been able to find her!"

"That is dire news," said the knight. "But I cannot await his return."

"Oh, my poor child!" wailed the woman. "Could you not look for her? They say there be dragons there!"

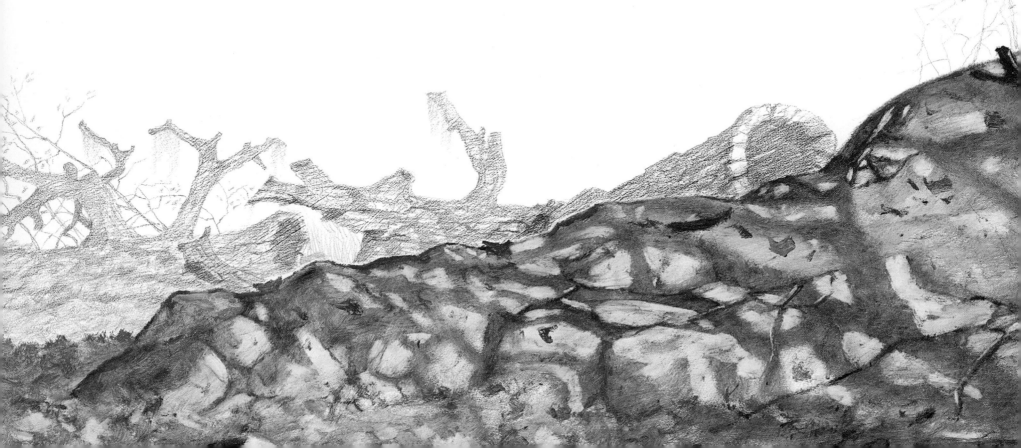

great conflict arose within the knight's heart. *Searching for lost children is hardly the work of a king's knight,* he thought. But still, he could not ignore her pleas.

Reluctantly he joined the searchers, and for two days they combed the vast forest. Then on the morning of the third day, the knight found little Bonnie safe in the care of a woodcutter's family.

With his rein repaired, the knight resumed his journey. One evening he happened upon the ruins of a wayside church and stopped to greet a monk who was mending a stone wall.

"God willing," said the monk, "I hope to finish rebuilding this church before I die. Finding… laborers…is…not…easy," he puffed, tugging at a large stone.

The knight clenched his jaw. *The duty of a knight is to defend churches, not mend them,* he thought.

Without a word, the knight galloped off. Dashing headlong at top speed, he tried to forget the image of the crumbling church. But in his heart the knight knew he had to turn back.

"I'll help you for a few days," he promised the monk.

The few days grew
into a few weeks. And the
weeks grew into months.
As the seasons came
and went, the knight
postponed his departure
again and again.

In the end, he stayed
until he helped the monk
place the last stained
glass window over the
door.

"It is finished," said
the knight.

The monk embraced him. "Without you, I could never have raised this church from its ruins. Great will be your reward someday." Tears glistened in the monk's eyes. "God bless you and keep you always."

Heartened by these words, the knight set out once more for the royal court. *Nothing will ever again stop me from reaching my King*, he vowed.

And the knight truly tried, but always there was someone who needed his help.

His mule he gave to a lame beggar.

His armor he bartered for books to assist a poor scholar.

His horse he sold to buy a serf's freedom.
But he could not part with his precious
golden spurs.

Many years passed, and the knight grew old and feeble. Then one cold winter's eve found him stumbling along a rough and lonely road. Blinded by the thick, falling snow, it would have been so easy for him to lie down and slip into a long, last sleep. But something deep inside would not allow the knight to give up, and as always, he pushed onward.

At last, the snow stopped and the moon slipped from behind
a heavy curtain of clouds. In the distance shimmered the most
magnificent vision the knight had ever seen.

"Surely this must be the castle of my King!" he cried. And
calling on his last bit of strength, he struggled on.

The next morning a rosy dawn spread over the castle. Near the drawbridge, a hunting party stopped to examine a heap of tattered rags.

"A beggar," said one hunter.

"Looks dead," said another.

"Throw him into the moat," said a third.

Just then, the heap of rags stirred. "Please, noble sirs," said the knight, struggling to his feet, "I have come to serve my King."

The hunters greeted his words with laughter and jeers.

With trembling hands, the knight frantically searched his rags, then held out his golden spurs.

At that moment, another rider approached. Everyone was silent as the man dismounted and carefully studied the spurs. "I have waited for you this long time," he finally said.

"Your Majesty!" the knight cried. He started to bow, but instead, slumped to the ground.

"Carry this noble knight to my chambers," commanded the King.

It was evening when the knight finally awoke. The King was sitting beside him, and in the doorway, someone was singing.

Gather round if you would hear
The wondrous tale I sing
Of a gallant knight who long ago
Set out to serve his King.

"My minstrel sings of your long and faithful service to me," said the King.

"His song cannot be about me," the knight whispered, "for I have never served you."

"Ah," said the King with a smile, "but you have. All these many years, tales of your gallant deeds have reached me. Did you not know that every time you helped one of my people, you were my own true and faithful knight?"

The knight closed his eyes. "Then I have not been an errant knight after all?" he whispered.

"Never," said the King. "And you shall wear these golden spurs once again as you ride by my side."

A faint smile touched the knight's lips. "My long journey has not been in vain," he said with a sigh.

"I have followed my heart *and* I have served my King."

ILLUMINATION
Arts

P.O. Box 1865 ◆ Bellevue, WA 98009
Tel: 425-644-7185 ◆ 888-210-8216 (orders only) ◆ Fax: 425-644-9274
www.illumin.com

Library of Congress Cataloging-in-Publication Data

Tompert, Ann.
   The errant knight / story by Ann Tompert ; illustrations by Doug Keith.
      p. cm.
   Summary: A knight on his way to serve his king is delayed, over and over again, by
people who need his help and he spends years struggling and hoping to finally reach the
royal castle and fulfill his duty.
   ISBN 0-9701907-6-X
   (1. Knights and knighthood—Fiction. 2. Conduct of life—Fiction.) I. Keith, Doug, ill. II.
Title.

PZ7.T598 Er 2003
(Fic)—dc21

2002027512

Published in the United States of America
Printed in Singapore by Tien Wah Press
Book Designer: Molly Murrah, Murrah & Company, Kirkland, WA

Illumination Arts Publishing Company, Inc.
A member of Publishers in Partnership—replanting our nation's forests

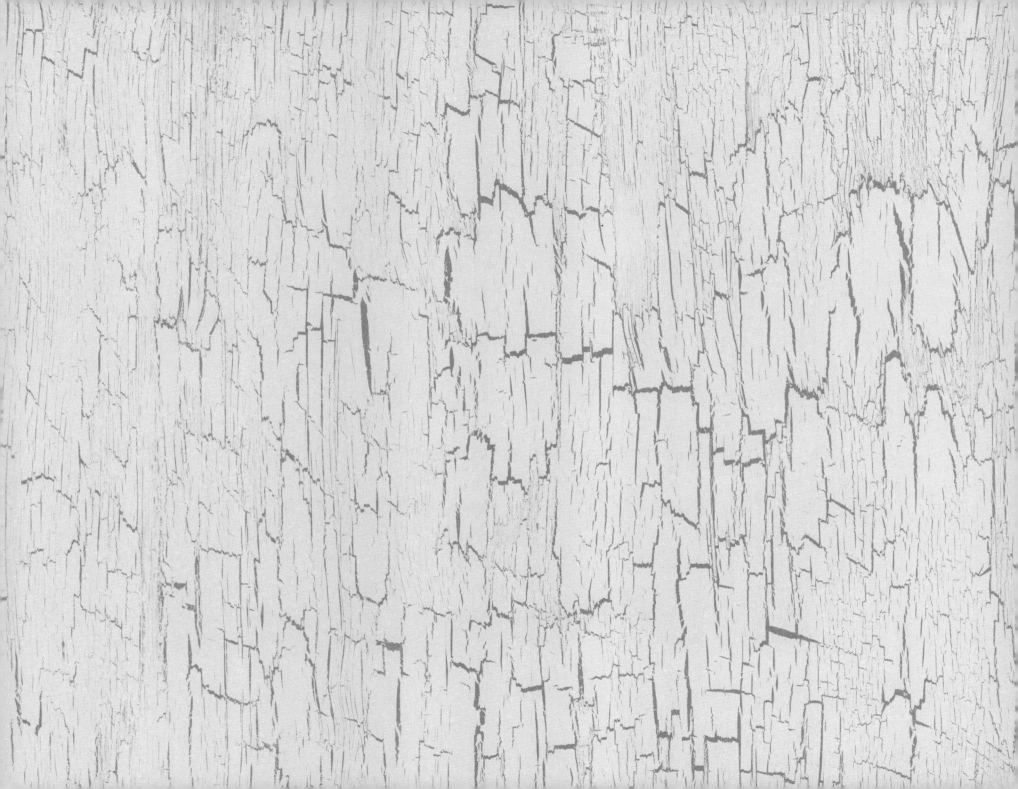